# A R___
# on the River

Written by Barbara Fletcher
Illustrated by Helen Humphries

A Tudor street scene.

# Contents

| | |
|---|---:|
| Tudor Family Tree | 4 |
| Introduction | 5 |
| A Very Special Bed | 11 |
| The Gathering Storm | 22 |
| A New Beginning | 31 |
| Measuring the Days | 42 |
| Friends in High Places | 56 |
| A Visit to the Tamars | 67 |
| Return of the Fool | 75 |
| Away into the Night | 85 |
| Dawn on the River | 93 |
| Secret Messages | 102 |
| Old Friends | 109 |
| Letters from Friends | 115 |
| Glossary | 124 |
| Bibliography | 126 |

# Tudor Monarchy 1485–1603

**Henry VII, King of England** (1457–1509) *married* **Elizabeth of York** (1466–1503)

## Children of Henry VII and Elizabeth of York

- **Arthur, Prince of Wales** (1486–1502)
- **Margaret** (1489–1541) *married* **James IV, King of Scotland** (1473–1513)
- **Henry VIII, King of England** (1491–1547)
- *Five other brothers and sisters*

## The Six Wives of Henry VIII

|  |  |  |
|---|---|---|
| Catherine of Aragon | (1485–1536) | married 1509 (divorced) |
| Anne Boleyn | (1500–1536) | married 1533 (executed) |
| Jane Seymour | (1507–1537) | married 1536 (died in childbirth) |
| Anne of Cleves | (1515–1557) | married 1540 (divorced) |
| Catherine Howard | (1525–1542) | married 1540 (executed) |
| Catherine Parr | (1512–1548) | married 1543 |

## Children of Henry VIII

- **Mary I** (1516–1558), became Queen of England 1553 — mother: Catherine of Aragon
- **Elizabeth I** (1533–1603), became Queen of England 1558 — mother: Anne Boleyn
- **Edward VI** (1537–1553), became King of England 1547 — mother: Jane Seymour

## Scottish Line

- **James IV, King of Scotland** (1473–1513) married **Margaret**
- **James V, King of Scotland** (1512–1542) *married* **Mary of Guise** (1515–1560)
- **Mary, Queen of Scots** (1542–1587) *married* **Henry Stuart, Lord Darnley** (1545–1566)
- **James VI, King of Scotland** (1566–1625)

# Introduction

## The Tudors

The first Tudor monarch of England was King Henry VII. He was a Welsh nobleman with a claim to the English throne through his mother, and Tudor was his family name. When he became king in 1485, after defeating King Richard III at the battle of Bosworth, he brought to an end thirty years of fighting between two rival branches of the English royal family. The rival branches were known as the Houses of York and Lancaster.

Henry belonged to the House of Lancaster, but he married Elizabeth of York (daughter of a former king of England) and so reunited the two factions. During the wars, the House of York had been represented by a white rose. The House of Lancaster was associated with a red rose. And so the fighting became known as the Wars of the Roses.

King Henry VII adopted as his symbol a rose that was both red and white – the Tudor Rose. It was the mark of royalty until the last of the Tudor monarchs, Henry's granddaughter,

Elizabeth Tudor, at the age of thirteen.
Painting by an unknown artist, c. 1546.

## Introduction

Elizabeth I. When she died, childless, in 1603, the throne passed to another branch of the royal family, the Stuarts.

The Tudors brought peace and prosperity to England. They defied all threats from Europe and rival claims to their throne. England's population grew, and by the end of Elizabeth's reign there were about four million people. Laws were more firmly and fairly enforced, trade thrived, and a growing class of merchants became rich and successful.

Some things didn't go quite so smoothly, however. Henry VII's son, Henry VIII, married six times, always hoping for a male heir. The result was just one son, the sickly Edward, whose mother was Henry's third wife, Jane Seymour. Edward became king at nine years of age and died at sixteen.

Henry had a daughter, Mary, by his first wife, Catherine of Aragon, but Catherine failed to produce a son, and Henry wished to be rid of her so that he could marry again. The Pope of the Roman Catholic Church refused to allow Henry to divorce and so he declared himself head of a new Church of England. English churchmen then gave him his divorce.

*Introduction*

In 1533 Henry's second wife, Anne Boleyn, disappointed him by giving birth to another daughter, the future Elizabeth I. No sons followed and, three years later, Henry had Anne executed for the crime of adultery. Had she given birth to a boy, no doubt things would have gone differently for her.

Because Henry's marriages to both their mothers had been declared invalid, Elizabeth and Mary were then known as the Lady Elizabeth and the Lady Mary, rather than as "Princess". But the sisters were always treated with respect and deference, because they were the daughters of the King.

Both Mary and Elizabeth lived to succeed their father as monarch after their brother Edward's death in 1553. During her five-year reign, Mary tried to take England back into the Roman Catholic Church, killing or persecuting many Protestants (as followers of the reformed churches came to be known).

Elizabeth followed Mary as queen in 1558, and returned to the Protestant form of worship. She ruled for forty-five years and became the greatest of the Tudor kings and queens – some say, of *all* England's kings and queens.

## Introduction

### A Rose on the River

Our story opens during the reign of Henry VIII, in the year of Elizabeth I's birth, and closes in 1545, when she was just twelve years old. Our other main characters – Robin, Thomas, and Elizabeth Tamar – are fictional, but there are some names taken from the pages of history. For example, the head of the Lady Elizabeth's household at Hatfield was Lady Bryan. Catherine Champernowne acted as Elizabeth's nurse and governess.

Also mentioned in these pages are King Henry's Secretary of State, Thomas Cromwell, and Eustace Chapuys, who was the London ambassador of the Holy Roman Emperor. At that time, the Emperor ruled Catholic Spain, as well as the Netherlands and large parts of Italy. Cromwell and Chapuys met in secret soon before the execution of Anne Boleyn (see page 53), and that meeting may have influenced the King's decision on his wife's fate. Henry's daughter Mary also communicated secretly with Chapuys for many years.

# Chapter One

## A Very Special Bed

Late August, 1533. The day had been sunny, and the sky was still clear and sharp. The river had an autumnal calm, carrying with it memories of sun-baked summer days. There was, as yet, no hint of the winter to come.

"The calm before the storm," said the boatman, lifting his weather-beaten face to the sky. He glanced at the young boy at his side. "Last drop of summer before the cold sets in."

The child watched and listened. He knew the older man well enough to wait for more.

*A Rose on the River*

The boatman returned his gaze to the sky. "Bright days and cold nights," he murmured, as if he were now unaware of his audience. "Freezing nights by Christmas, and then look out!"

"What shall I look out for, Uncle?" said the boy, trying to read the wrinkled face for a clue of what was to come.

"Look out for thyself, boy, that's what! Look out for thy kith and kin and make sure there's wood on the fire and food in thy belly. There's many a young 'un died o' cold on a winter's night, with no cover on 'is back and no food in 'is belly."

They made an odd pair: the ferryman with his gnarled, work-worn fingers and the young boy, no more than nine years old, but eager to learn.

Thomas Smythe had started life some forty-eight years before, in a village on the edge of the city of London. His father was a village blacksmith who earned a good living from the farmers working the local fields and those passing through on their way to the city. The weary travellers would stop to have their horses shod and to refresh themselves at the

## A Very Special Bed

inn, where Mistress Lucy would delight them with foaming ale and steaming pastry pies full of turnips and onions.

Thomas would have followed his father into the trade, had his older brothers not been there first. He was one of seven sons. Fourteen children had been born to the blacksmith and his wife, but the family had lost four of them, born dead or dead within a month of their birth and that was only to be expected. Life was hard for most, and you were lucky to survive your early years and even luckier to live beyond the age of forty-five. A poor harvest and a bitter winter could wipe out the population of whole villages. The young and the old died first.

The year that Thomas was born, a new king, Henry Tudor, had marched victoriously into London. With him came the peace and prosperity in which the boy had grown, and an end to the civil war that had raged through England and Wales, snatching farmers and their sons from orchard and field and leaving them dead or wounded far from their homes.

The young Welsh King had united the warring royal families by marrying Elizabeth of

*A Rose on the River*

York and combining the red and white roses of the two houses, York and Lancaster. King Henry's new Tudor rose – red with a white centre – was an image to be carried, copied, worn, and drawn throughout England.

Thomas was eleven years old when he set off along the country lanes, bound for the city of London. He had the clothes he stood up in and a fine pair of leather lace-up shoes, made for him by his older brother Ben, who was apprentice to the shoemaker in the village.

Thomas found work on the barges, a regular, bustling trade, ferrying passengers along and between the muddy banks of the River Thames. London's streets were then crowded, filthy, and often dangerous. There was, as yet, only one bridge across the river – London Bridge – and it, too, was narrow, dark, and crammed with shops and houses. The watermen and their fleets of sturdy wooden boats did a thriving business with travellers who had good reason to avoid the roads.

Work on the river meant rising at dawn and sleeping on the boat, or in a warehouse at the riverside if you were really lucky, or the river was frozen. Thomas soon mastered the art of

## A Very Special Bed

helping customers in and out of the barge and occasionally fishing them out of the river if they had drunk too much ale in the taverns.

The river had been Thomas' life, and now he was ready to teach his nephew, Robin. For years he had felt an ache in his bones and a stiffness in his joints made worse by the damp wooden boat, the murky river mists, and the foul stench of city life that hung over the river bank, especially in hot weather.

Thomas' eyes were also beginning to fail him, so it was Robin who spotted the riverboat and its passenger.

"Look! Over there, Uncle!" He pointed to a small boat further out in the river, occupied by a stout figure resting confidently on his oars, waving and shouting.

"Ahoy, Thomas," the voice sounded across the water. "I'm coming alongside!"

Within minutes, his oars were churning in the tidal current around the ferryboat and a rope was thrown for Robin to tie up on the bank. The afternoon's quiet stillness was gone and a new excitement took its place.

"Bless me, Thomas, if I ain't seen it all!" gasped the newcomer, as he hauled himself into their boat, setting it rocking and spilling river water down onto the bottom boards.

"Good day to ye, Master Tamar," shouted Thomas, putting one hand out to help steady the visitor while trying to balance the boat by holding the ropes tightly in his other.

"Bless me if I ain't…" Master Tamar stopped to regain his breath and wipe his brow with a large red cloth. For a few seconds, Robin had a chance to study him. Master Tamar looked to be about the same age as Thomas, though the years had certainly been kinder to him. His face was round and ruddy, his eyes were darting blue sapphires, and his mouth, although almost toothless, was drawn into a wide grin. As he explained to them just what he had seen, his ample chest rose and fell rapidly, and Robin recognized the smell of ale on his breath.

"I was up by Westminster there, checking on the boats and doing a bit of business, when what should I see but a crowd gathering around the Treasury and a lot of shouting and calling out and such."

Thomas offered his friend a leather flask, from which he took a swig before continuing.

## A Very Special Bed

"I pulled the boat over, right close by the landing there, and bless me, Thomas, if I didn't see the King himself!"

Robin's eyes widened and he drew nearer. He had seen Master Tamar before, passing up and down on the river. He was an old friend of his Uncle Thomas and the two men had shared much talk and ale together over the years. Master Tamar had come originally from Cornwall, although Robin had no notion of the whereabouts of that county, except that it was many miles from London. Master Tamar's family had worked on the River Tamar there, and he had taken his name from it when, as a child, he had come with his father to work on the River Thames.

The Tamars had brought boats with them and had, in time, become rich and well known on the river. Many men worked for them, ferrying people and cargo. Now Master Tamar's father was gone, and his son had long since settled into wealth, influence, and respectability.

Still, Master Tamar loved the river, and those he had known on it in his youth. Robin did not know how he and Thomas had become friends, but he knew that they were always glad to be in each other's company. It was one of the few times that Thomas laughed, and Robin loved to hear it, although he often did not understand the joke.

"And what is Old Hal up to now?" asked Thomas, sipping from the flask himself.

"Who is Old Hal?" said Robin, realizing too late that the two men had forgotten he was there and did not want to be interrupted.

"The King, boy, the King!" snapped Thomas without looking at Robin.

"King Henry VIII – our Sovereign Lord," said Master Tamar, with genuine pride in his voice.

"And Prince of the Church now, too," added Thomas sourly. He surprised Robin, then, by spitting with disgust into the river.

There was a moment's silence before Master Tamar, not wishing to begin a debate on a subject that was dividing the country, continued with the story.

"He was overseeing the loading of a very precious cargo onto one of the royal barges."

"Oh aye!" sighed Thomas. "More jewels and gold coinage for the new Queen?"

"Nay indeed, my friend. Thou wouldst never guess in all thy dreams what was loaded on

## A Very Special Bed

yon barge. If I had not seen it with these trusty eyes of mine, I..."

"Get on with it, Master. What did ye see on the barge this day?" urged Thomas, laughing in spite of his exasperation.

"A bed!" declared Master Tamar, and his eyes darted from one to the other of his listeners, brimming with amusement.

"A bed? The great King Harry troubles himself to see a bed put on a barge!" exclaimed Thomas, beginning to laugh again.

"Aye indeed, sir, but not just any bed. When all the commotion was done, and the bed safely stowed, the King rode away and I made it my business to row alongside the barge itself. I was silent and stealthy, like a gracious swan." At this, he broke off again and roared with laughter, and Thomas and Robin laughed with him.

"I shouted up to one of the hands, and he said the bed is bound for the palace at Greenwich. The new Queen Anne – or Nan Bullen, as she was not long since – is about to bring forth Henry's son, our new Prince. She is to have a wondrous bed that was given to the King by a French prince. The King says she

*A Rose on the River*

must have the best of everything and it must be taken to Greenwich Palace and prepared for her lying-in."

Only then did the visitor relax and, for the first time, the little ferryboat regained some stability on the uneasy river current.

"Well, well," said Thomas. "What think ye of that, young Robin?"

Robin did not have time to answer before Master Tamar began afresh.

"And I am here to tell thee, Thomas, that the barge is travelling slowly and will be coming this way in the next hour, shouldst thou wish to see yon glorious bed for thyself!"

And so it was that young Robin, the ferry boy, was witness to a special bed on its journey to Greenwich Palace for a long-awaited royal birth. King Henry had moved heaven and earth to receive this child, who was confidently expected to be a son and heir. He had declared himself supreme head of a new Church of England when the head of the Catholic Church, Pope Clement, had refused to divorce him from his first wife, Catherine of Aragon.

## A Very Special Bed

Now English churchmen had declared Henry's marriage to Catherine null and void, and Anne Boleyn (nicknamed Nan Bullen by the people, with whom she was not popular) was crowned Queen of England. The child of Henry and his new wife was born on September 7, 1533, in the royal bed at Greenwich Palace. It was a safe delivery, but no prince was born.

That night, the River Thames was cold. The wind blew hard from the east, making the ferryboats dance on the water. Thomas had spoken that day of the calm before the storm, and he had been wiser than he could have known. The expectant calm of autumn was about to give way to a winter of bitter disappointment and disaster.

# Chapter Two

## The Gathering Storm

November, 1533. The disappointment that had clouded the land and enraged the King gave way to resignation and hope that there was still time for Queen Anne to give the King a son and heir. Word had spread quickly among the river folk of the King's rage and the Queen's tears when the Princess was born. For them, the birth of a healthy child was good news, but the King had cancelled the special celebrations that the birth of a Tudor prince would have brought. Plans for tournaments and jousting were abandoned, and the royal christening was a rich but quiet affair.

It was bad news for the river trade. The ferryboats would have been busy for days carrying revellers and sightseers up and down the river. A disappointed Robin had been longing to see the people dressed up in their best. He wanted to ride the river when the old city was trimmed in scarlet, green, and gold.

Still, once the rush of harvest produce to the markets was over, life for Robin had been easy. Despite Thomas' warnings, the weather had been fairly mild and, when the storm came that Friday night, it was unexpected. The boatmen were caught off guard.

"Robin, tie the boat now," said Thomas. "They're all in their beds for the night."

This was one of Thomas' favourite expressions and a signal to Robin that work was over for the day. But it was unlike Thomas not to look up at the sky and read the night like a priest reading a sacred book. It was unusual for him not to raise his grey head as the wind blew up from the estuary and to sniff the sea breeze like an animal seeking the scent of its prey.

"'Twas the workings of fate that old Tom missed the signs," Master Tamar said often in the months that followed.

The truth of it was that Thomas was tired, and the relentless dull ache in his arthritic knees and fingers made him want to leave the boat forever to lie in a golden field under the sun. Sometimes, when the damp wooden boat lay cold against his back, he imagined he was back in the August cornfields of home, whispering with his friends about the noon daydreams of childhood.

Thomas had been worn down by the river's changing moods and the foul river mists that cut deep into his lungs. He was getting old and his desire to rest made him careless that night. He did not take the boat to a safer mooring.

Robin's first memory of the storm was the sound of the east wind roaring up the river like a frightened animal, sending whatever was not nailed or tied down into spasms of frantic movement. The river jerked the ferryboat with sharp slaps of water against its sides and Robin awoke, startled and afraid. But it was only the first flash of lightning that broke Thomas' dream and forced his stiff body into action.

*The Gathering Storm*

From that point on, Robin's memories were a series of frightening images. The river came alive like a great serpent trying to fling the boats from its back, twisting and straining to escape the river's banks. People clung to their boats and shouted instructions, warnings, and cries for help against the noise of the wind. Many further downriver had seen the weather change and were now pulling their boats to safety across the river bank or lifting them over the stone steps. Their bodies were lit up by regular flashes of lightning and Robin saw them bent double under the sound of crashing thunder, as if it were wielding a stick across their backs.

Along many parts of the river, the buildings came right down to the water's edge, and there Robin saw children being passed from the boats to people leaning from the windows. For many, it was too late, as a downpour of rain swelled the river and flooded the plain.

Thomas scrambled clear of the heaving boat as it came close to flinging itself onto the river bank. There he turned to call to his bewildered nephew. "Robin, leave the boat, boy! Get out of it now!" But his words were lost in the noise of the storm and the chaos of the river.

With Robin still aboard, the small ferryboat was torn from its moorings and tossed far into the river, where it rode on the back of the water like a child trying to tame a wild horse.

When it started to sink, Robin could still see Thomas' frantic face mouthing words to him from the shore, but he could hear nothing but the savage blast of wind in his ears. He remembered being thrown into the water and the shock like ice around his ribs.

Robin swam with fear and fury, not stopping when broken branches and the nameless debris of the river smashed into his shoulders or tore into his face. He swam for his life and, when he reached the river's edge, he was dragged across the mud to safety by two welcome arms. He could not see or grasp them, but he felt their warmth and, strangely, even through the storm, he was soothed by their sweet scent of lavender and rose.

It was many hours before Robin was aware of anything, but, when his brain told his body it had rested enough, he woke to the same lingering scent of the previous night. He was

*The Gathering Storm*

greatly shocked, therefore, when he gingerly opened his eyes to see the robust, grinning face of Master Tamar greeting him.

"Damn my eyes, if it ain't Thomas Smythe's young 'un!" he exclaimed excitedly. "I thought I knew that face!"

"Edward, please, mind thy language in front of the children." The lady who spoke so softly but firmly was standing just behind Master Tamar. From her age and manner, Robin guessed that this must be his wife, Mistress Tamar.

Then another voice made Robin's head turn quickly on the white linen pillow.

"Thomas Smythe, Father? Who is he?" The voice belonged to a young girl standing at the side of the bed. Her head was covered in a cream-coloured cap that encircled her innocent face and tried in vain to control the mass of black curls that escaped from its lace edges. She was probably close to Robin's age, but her fair skin and freshly laundered clothes told him that she had lived a very different life.

Robin tried to focus on her bright young features, but he was forced to shut his eyes tightly as a searing pain shot across his brow.

As he lifted his hand, his fingers met with a thick wad of linen wrapped around his head. Inside the bandage was a parcel of healing herbs – comfrey and rosemary, among others. He knew that he had been saved from the storm, but, before he had managed to thank his rescuers, or ask after his uncle, sleep overcame him once more.

Over the next few weeks, Robin gradually regained his strength and health under the watchful eye of Mistress Tamar and her daughter, Elizabeth. Of Master Tamar he saw little. Business on the river kept him away from home for most of the day. The storm had wrecked many boats and barges. With his boat-building connections in Cornwall and his many contacts along the Thames, Master Tamar was fully and profitably occupied helping to rebuild the water trade. There was no news of Thomas and no one spoke of him in the house, for fear of upsetting Robin. The ferryboat, of course, had been lost and so, no doubt, had Thomas. The future, Robin knew, was too awful to contemplate, and so he didn't!

Every time his mind drifted to thoughts of his dear uncle or the terrors of the storm, he turned the memories away and made the most of his new life with the Tamars, which he knew could not last. Meanwhile, he was happy to have the comfort of a soft, warm bed and to be woken with a platter of fresh bread and cheese.

Robin quickly discovered that Mistress Tamar had not been well since the birth of Elizabeth, and that there were a number of servants in the house to help her. The Mistress doted on her only child and had taught her to read and write – a skill that Elizabeth had begun to share with Robin, although he had no notion of how it would benefit a ferry boy.

No doubt, if Master Tamar had not been so preoccupied with his business interests, Robin's stay would have been shorter. However, seeing his wife and daughter so happy and young Robin lending a hand around the house, Master Tamar turned a blind eye and thought of his good friend Thomas, who, he felt sure, must have been lost on the night of the storm.

And so winter turned into spring, and life was good for Robin and for Elizabeth Tamar. But now, further along the river at Greenwich, another Elizabeth was making her presence felt. The new year was to bring changes for her and her mother, Queen Anne. The storms of November had passed, but angry clouds still gathered over London and, as King Henry took pleasure in his new daughter, he brooded on the son he had been denied.

# Chapter Three

## A New Beginning

January, 1534. The first three months of Princess Elizabeth's life were spent at Greenwich with her mother, although, as was the custom of the time, she was given to a wet nurse to be fed and cared for. It was important that the Queen be able to resume her royal duties as soon as possible, and these precious months when Elizabeth could have been cradled in her mother's arms were spent largely in the company of others. This was to be the pattern of the next three years for

Elizabeth Tudor, and so the baby Princess was left with very few memories of her mother.

King Henry was happy to show a public pride in his daughter. She had inherited the auburn hair and pale complexion of the Tudors, so unlike the raven tresses and almond-shaped eyes of her mother. She was named Elizabeth after King Henry's own mother, and it soon became clear that she had also inherited the quick brain and many talents of her father.

At three months old, the baby Princess was taken away from the danger and disease of the city to Hatfield, some twenty miles north of London. There Elizabeth had her own household under the care of Lady Bryan. Her older sister, Mary, now seventeen years old, was also sent to live at Hatfield, as one of Elizabeth's ladies-in-waiting.

Indignantly, Mary refused to recognize Elizabeth as a royal princess, saying that she alone was the Princess, although her father had ordered that she now be addressed as the Lady Mary. It was not always a happy household.

## A New Beginning

Hatfield was surrounded by Hatfield Forest, a majestic woodland that was a favourite hunting ground for Henry and his court. They could often be seen galloping along the open chases that criss-crossed the forest and formed broad ridges between the oak and beech trees.

Near the centre of the forest was a lake surrounded by marshland, and at the side of this lake there sat a grey-haired man in a small fishing boat. He heard the wheels of carriages passing through the forest, and the occasional laughter and music of servants and men-at-arms. He heard the clatter of horses' hoofs and wondered idly if they would need to be shod in the nearby village, where his brother was blacksmith. But he did not want to be reminded of London and its royal masters.

The banks of the Thames, and the city that clustered along them, held sad memories for him. He had left it all behind, along with a part of himself that was lost one stormy night. Also lost that night, or so he believed, was the life of his young nephew. For this he blamed himself. After bearing the bad news to his family, he had taken himself deep into the forest, where he passed his days silently, living off the land.

As Elizabeth Tudor was settling into the countryside at Hatfield, Elizabeth Tamar was at home in London with her new friend and pupil, Robin. But at last there came a day when Master Tamar called Robin to his chamber with the news that their happy time together was shortly to end. Robin must leave.

"I should have known this would happen," cried Elizabeth when Robin told her the news. "I will speak to my father and beg that thou might stay!"

"'Tis no use, Elizabeth," replied Robin. "The Master and Mistress have shown great kindness to me, though I am but a stranger to them. I must earn my keep now that Thomas is gone."

"Wouldst thou rather go back to thy family or stay in London?" she asked at last, her eyes glassy with tears and her round face sadder than Robin had ever seen it.

"I cannot go back on my own. I would never find the village without Thomas to lead me."

## A New Beginning

Now Robin's eyes also shone with tears as he spoke of his uncle.

"Anyway, Master Tamar has found me work on one of his new barges on the river. It's work I know, and I can earn my keep and repay thy father for his kindness."

Elizabeth turned and ran from the room. Robin could hear her crying for a long time that night as darkness closed over the house. He remembered the night he was brought there and his first sight of Elizabeth Tamar. It was she who had dragged him up the river bank, straining her arms until her muscles screamed for relief. She had braved the storm with her family, as many living near the Thames had done, leaving their homes to wade into the water to provide help and shelter for those who had lost their livelihoods that night.

Elizabeth Tamar was only eight years old, but children grew up quickly then, even in the richest households, and she already knew she must be strong to survive. Her soft skin, bobbing curls, and velvet gowns were just the outside trappings. Inside, Elizabeth Tamar was fearless and brave. Just like the royal

*A Rose on the River*

Elizabeth, she had inherited many qualities from her father: understanding beyond her years, a quick brain, and the flair for business that was even now making her family one of the richest on the river. Life was full of promise for the two Elizabeths that year.

For Robin, the spring brought a return to work. It was with sadness in his heart that he bade farewell to the Tamars and made his way from the comfortable merchants' quarter through the cobbled streets to the river. The tall houses, wider at the top than on the lower floors, seemed to lean unsteadily over him as he walked through the narrow streets. Had they wanted to, the occupants could have reached out and touched one another through the upstairs windows. The lower level of some of the houses was used to shelter animals. In others, it was used as a shop. Signs hung from the timber frames to show passers-by what was on sale. From the shuttered windows came a confusion of smells and sounds as the daily routine of buying and selling brought life to the side streets of London.

## A New Beginning

Although it was early morning, the streets were busy and Robin was jostled and pushed repeatedly. From time to time, he had to duck as showers of night slops rained down from upstairs windows with little or no warning. Underfoot, the streets were heaped with household waste and discarded rubbish.

Master Tamar had given Robin careful instructions and directions to his new place of work, slipping a silver coin into his hand for good luck. In the pocket of his jerkin was a chunk of bread and a little goat cheese wrapped in a red kerchief by the Mistress herself. The jerkin had once belonged to the Master and was worn in places, but Elizabeth and one of the maidservants had sat in the evenings and stitched and patched until it fitted Robin's slight figure. They assured him that he looked quite the gentleman in the altered jerkin, with hose to match. It was with a strong sense of satisfaction that he rounded the corner to the wharf.

Within seconds of seeing it, Robin felt a push from behind, and barely glimpsed a leg stretched out in front of him before he tumbled to the ground, banging his head hard on the cobbles. Two boys, older and broader than Robin, had tripped him up, and they now began to roll him across the ground, shouting for money. Robin kicked out and struggled, but they were masters of their art. Within a few minutes, they had wrenched the coin from his fist and found the food in his pocket. After making sure he had nothing else worth stealing, they ran off towards the market stalls, disappearing into a group of apprentices playing football with a pig's bladder and losing themselves among the market traders.

Shaken, Robin sat for a while brushing the dust and mud from his clothes and dabbing blood from his knees through the torn holes in his hose. He wiped his running nose with the back of his hand and only then realized that his nose was bleeding and hurt when he touched it.

"Here, fool, use this!" said a voice from behind him.

Robin whipped around like a frightened rabbit, expecting to suffer another blow.

"It's all right, young fool," said the voice again. "Wipe thy nose and get thyself up, or a greater fool than the Fool's fool wilt thou be."

## A New Beginning

Robin gaped in surprise at the figure who addressed him. Was it a man or a boy? Robin could not be sure. He was tall and slim and dressed from head to foot in scarlet and gold. He wore a tunic with an alternating red and yellow diamond pattern, and hose striped in the same hues. On his head was a curious hat with three horn-shaped protrusions, each tipped by a small circular bell that jingled as he moved. His feet were strapped into pointed leather shoes, also equipped with bells, and in his left hand he carried a small stick with a horse's head carved on the handle. He was holding out a small square of cloth.

Robin stared rudely at him and his mouth must have hung open in amazement, for the voice spoke again. "Why is it that thy mouth hangs so?" At this, the figure pulled his own mouth into a great dim-witted grin.

"And why do thy knees knock like this?" he continued, making an even sillier face and bending his legs so that his knees knocked together in a ridiculous way.

He looked so strange and yet so merry that Robin, gashed and torn though he was, started to laugh.

"That's better, young master." The voice was soft and friendly. "Do not let thyself be tricked by yon knaves next time. The streets of London are full of rogues. Pray, keep the cloth and pass it on, for, sure as I am the King's Fool, what goes around comes around. Farewell, young sir, and think of me."

As quickly as he had appeared, the Fool was gone. Robin watched him make his way through the stalls until he reached the market square, where he joined a group of players. They shouted greetings to him and almost immediately the play began, with Robin's benefactor somersaulting his way from one side of the square to the other, to the whistles and applause of the audience.

Dazed and uncertain, Robin turned to face the river. He felt tempted to stay and watch the play, perhaps even join the group of players and travel on with them to the next town or city.

But that was just a dream. Robin knew the risks of being alone on the streets with an empty stomach and no roof over his head. He must find the barge and begin his new life. He had been offered work and he must do his

*A New Beginning*

best. He owed Master Tamar that much, and, of course, he owed it to the memory of his poor dead uncle.

Robin shivered. With a heavy heart, he made his way to the wharf.

# Chapter Four

## Measuring the Days

Autumn, 1535. Working for Master Tamar was quite different from the life Robin had known with Thomas. He worked the river in much the same way, ferrying passengers from dawn to sunset, but he had sleeping quarters with several other young boatmen in one of the warehouses, and every Sunday afternoon was his own. He did not see much of the Master, who became richer every year, judging by the fine clothes he wore, but, surprisingly, he remained friends with Elizabeth Tamar.

Whenever she came to market with one of the servants, they would take the ferry home so that she could spend some time with Robin. Master Tamar usually spent Sunday afternoon in bed, after a sumptuous meal of fine meats and poultry (the poor man's fare of vegetables was not for him). Mistress Tamar took the opportunity to invite Robin to the house, and so, whenever the weather was fine enough, he would walk the two miles across the city to spend an hour or two with his friends.

These were the happiest times of his life. Mistress Tamar was a kind woman who would have loved a large family. She fussed over Robin on his visits, giving him sweetmeats, stitching his clothes, and sometimes filling the wooden water tub in the yard for him, so that he could wash away the city grime.

"Pray, what hast thou there, Elizabeth?" asked Robin one day, as the girl arrived on the ferry with her maid. Elizabeth Tamar was clutching a small leather-bound book, beautifully decorated with lettering that Robin could not read at all.

"Why, 'tis a prayer book, Robin, that Father hath purchased for me. Dost thou wish to look?" She handed Robin the book, and he carefully opened the thick cover.

"'Tis no use, Elizabeth, I cannot read the script." He looked at her with shame and embarrassment in his eyes.

"I have failed thee, Elizabeth, for I remember naught of what I learned with thee. The words are like a cipher to me. There is not one among them I can read."

At this, Elizabeth's round face, which looked no older than when they had first met, shone with amusement and she laughed aloud, showing her perfect teeth and dimpled cheeks. She was the prettiest thing Robin had ever seen, and it hurt him that she should make fun of him like this.

"Do not jest like that at my expense. Such a thing becomes thee not!" he snapped angrily.

"Oh, Robin, I would not laugh at thee!" Elizabeth smiled and put her soft white hand over his work-worn one. She leaned towards him in the boat and again he recognized the familiar scent of lavender and rose that was always with her.

"No wonder thou canst not read it, Robin, for the words are all in Latin."

"Of what use is that?" he asked, still uneasy and awkward.

"Why, to pray with, of course!" she replied and started to laugh again.

When Robin visited the house the following Sunday, Mistress Tamar brought up the subject of Robin's reading skills. It was obvious that mother and daughter had been discussing the events on the ferry earlier that week. Very tactfully, as was her way, the Mistress suggested that during his visits they might spend half an hour together in study.

"I know thy mother means the best for me, Elizabeth," said Robin later, as they walked in the garden, "but, honest and true, I shall forget all this learning when I get back to the river, and I durst not be caught idling with books on the ferry."

Elizabeth was quiet, knowing that he spoke the truth. "Fare thee well, Robin, and leave the matter with me."

---

Elizabeth Tamar was a clever girl. Before long, she had persuaded her father that it would be a good thing if a daily written record of ferry

*A Rose on the River*

passengers were kept. It would be, she said, a log to keep track of who was boarding the boat, the name of the destination, and how much money was paid.

"I've no time for that tomfoolery, girl, even if I had the boys to read and write. What nonsense thou dost dream!" was Master Tamar's first response. Indeed, such a thing was unheard of at a time when most people could neither read nor write, unless they belonged to the Church, or were rich enough to have a tutor.

His final words were different. "Very well, little scallywag. If Robin can do the job, we'll try the log on the long barge that goes the length of the river. That's the finest barge I have, and kept for gentry and the like. They will think highly of Master Tamar, who has boys as can read and write to work for him!"

It made good sense to Master Tamar to keep the log once he knew Robin already had the skills. He would have a tight check on the money changing hands, and he would also have a chance to impress the best-paying customers on the river. In fact, it suited everyone, and particularly Robin, who could now practise his reading and writing every day.

Life became easier for Robin in other ways, too. The barge carried passengers over long distances. Once they were boarded and the log completed, Robin was often left with time to spare as the boat glided through the muddy Thames. To pass the time, he had the idea of keeping a diary. He would sit at a table tucked away on the barge, so that the passengers hardly noticed he was there. As they talked together during the journey, Robin listened, and made notes on what happened and what was said during the day.

It began as a kind of game – matching names in the log to faces, then listening for clues and trying to guess the occupations of the passengers and the reasons for their journey. He was eavesdropping, certainly, but it was all quite harmless, and might have stayed that way had not fate intervened again.

The seasons were about to change and with them the fortunes of those in high places. Robin might have lived his life unaware of these events, but among his passengers were people with important contacts in the city: businessmen, churchmen, and servants. But these were not servants of the kind that the

Tamars employed. They were royal servants, servants with access to the court, and servants with access to the King!

The diary entries were simple enough at first.

*October 2nd, 1535*
Full barge every journey this day. Weather fair. Merchants taken from the Strand up to Hampton Court.

Very soon, however, the business and news of the travellers began to fill the diary:

*October 12th, 1535*
High tide and river foul. A former maidservant to the Good Queen Catherine, as she once was, on the barge today with her sister. Heard as how the Good Queen is removed to Kimbolton Castle in Huntingdon.

*October 13th, 1535*
Quiet day. Carried the maidservant's sister back to Greenwich. Heard her tell as how the

King's Fool made a jest in praise of the Good Queen and against Queen Anne. The Fool hath been sorely punished. Methinks this could be that same Fool who helped me on the wharf this year past.

*November 28th, 1535*

River mist means slow going this day. Bore a priest and a merchant from Hampton Court down to Greenwich. Rumours of the King's discontent with Queen Anne. His eye is said to be resting on a Seymour.

*December 3rd, 1535*

Goodly wind this day, but barge sluggardly due to waste from the fair in the river again. Gave passage to revellers travelling back to Greenwich. Great joy, as the Queen is said to be with child again. Princess Elizabeth removed from Hatfield to Hunsdon till the New Year.

It was clear from the diary that Robin was becoming more and more interested in his passengers and the news they brought with them. His reading and writing were now excellent, and whenever he saw Elizabeth they would go through the diary together.

At first, Robin would read his work aloud, then she would check the writing for spelling and punctuation. Robin learned so quickly, however, that soon he and Elizabeth would spend the time discussing the gossip and passengers on the boat. It was of great interest to them both.

He found that he was looking out for regular travellers and paying particular attention to those he knew to have fascinating stories of the King and his court. They, of course, had no interest in a barge boy and were completely oblivious to his skills and the parts they were playing in his diary.

The New Year brought an intensity to Robin's life that was reflected in the diary.

*January 14th, 1536*
*An air of sadness on the river today, for Good Queen Catherine is dead. She hath been dead a week at Kimbolton, the King not with her, nor*

has he seen her these past five years. Her body lies in the chapel, there watched over by three ladies of the household, one among them named Blanche. I am to check the log, for I am certain sure it was a maidservant named Blanche on the barge this autumn last.

*January 30th, 1536*

Master Seymour and two merchants aboard this day from Greenwich up to Kingston. Great commotion as the King hath taken a fall from his horse and the Queen's Majesty, so upset they say from the grief and worry, hath miscarried her child. They moved to the stern and were heads together an hour or more, but I was called to check for ice in the river and heard no more of what they said.

*February 12th, 1536*

Ice to the west but free from Hampton on. Made three visits to Greenwich this day, one to carry four foreign gentlemen with golden rings and fine velvet gowns. One had a great ruby set in gold on his middle finger and gave me a groat for my trouble. I understood not a word of what they jabbered, but they were secretive and watchful. They were not at the palace above an hour before the call came to take them back. When they came aboard, I heard one gentleman's name: Signor Chapuys. The others stepped aside for him and bowed low when he left the barge.

## February 20th, 1536

Elizabeth rode with us this day and said she hath heard from a merchant and his wife that the court is greatly excited, as the Queen is out of favour and there is talk that the King plots against her. We believe it is because there are no sons yet living. The merchant's wife says as how Nan Bullen is a witch and tricked the King's Majesty into marrying her when he should have stayed with Good Queen Catherine. Elizabeth says it is treason to speak so and the merchant's wife should mend her words. It put me in mind of Thomas and how he spat in the river when the King's annulment was touched on these three years past.

## March 31st, 1536

Called out late this night and told not to fill out the log. It was Chapuys, the Spanish gentleman with the ruby ring, alone at first and then joined by another passenger at Tower Wharf. I am beset by nerves and dread, for I am told that he was the King's man, Thomas Cromwell, and that I should never speak a word of what I have seen this night.

## April 5th, 1536

The Spanish gentlemen rode the river again and this time they were laughing and in high spirits. Master Tamar was with us this day and remarked on how Elizabeth hath become friendly with cousins of Lady Bryan, head of household to the Princess Elizabeth at Hatfield. He is very proud and pleased with his daughter and spent the journey talking of her easy way with Latin and French and Spanish, and of how she can draw and dance like an angel. I was surprised, as I know she is an angel, but she hath said nothing of these friends, or of French and Spanish. It seems to me that there is much about her I do not know, and yet she knows all of my small world.

*May Day, 1536*
Great celebrations. The King held a tournament at Greenwich and the river was crowded with vessels of many kinds. All were minded to join in the fun and take a view of the jousting from the bank. Friends of Lord Rochford travelled with us after and said as there was great fussing when the King left the tournament unexpectedly, without even telling the Queen.

*May 2nd, 1536*
My heart is heavy. Watched from the berth this day as Queen Anne was taken by river from Greenwich to the Tower. All the barges were silent as she passed, and then we followed the procession for a full two hours till we reached

the Barbican Gate. Even now I am filled with dread when I think on how she began screaming at the sight of the Tower. She looked so small, with her raven black hair and her pale, thin face. The Constable of the Tower, Sir William Kingston, went up to her, and I thought that she had swooned, but he seemed to comfort her and she began to climb the stairs. I swear I never thought to see this day, but the Queen of England fell to her knees on the stairs and cried. Then they helped her up and she went through the Court Gate. I wish I could tell Elizabeth of this, but she hath gone away this month or more to stay with the Bryan family, and I have no one else to tell save this diary. God spare us all, but this is a night of shame for England.

# Chapter Five

## Friends in High Places

The shame continued when, at eight in the morning on Friday, May 19, 1536, Anne Boleyn was led out to Tower Green and executed before a small group, including Thomas Cromwell. It was not through the ferry passengers that Robin learned the details of this tragic event, but from Elizabeth Tamar. Her visits to Robin were now fewer, and he felt he could no longer make his Sunday visits to the household as he once did. More often than not, Elizabeth was away when he called anyway, visiting the Bryans or the Poles or some other high-sounding family. Robin was welcomed by the Tamar staff, who continued to increase in number, but he soon realized that Elizabeth's life had changed and that he was no longer a part of it.

In the autumn of 1536, however, Robin received a short note from Elizabeth asking him to come to the house the following Sunday. She had, she said, great news for him. When he arrived, he was surprised to see the servants packing away the family belongings into sturdy trunks and storing breakables in boxes of straw.

"Oh, Robin, I am so pleased to see thee!" Elizabeth ran towards Robin with a face flushed with excitement and pleasure. Robin's heart leaped when he saw that she had not changed towards him, despite his fears.

"Prithee, come and tell me all thy news. Art thou well?" She grasped his hand and pulled him into the main chamber of the house, where Mistress Tamar sat by the fire looking thinner and paler than he remembered her.

"Nay, it is not I who hath news. Life on the river is the same as ever. What of thee? What events are these?" Robin gestured towards the packing cases and trunks.

It was Mistress Tamar who spoke. "We are removing, Robin, but come to me first, so that I can see thy dear face. I have missed thee this last year. Come sit with me."

Robin came to her willingly. She looked frail, and he felt guilty that he had not kept up his weekly visits to the house.

Elizabeth took up the story. "Father is to retire with Mother to the country, Robin. They have a wondrous house with land and stables, and there must be over a score of servants to do I know not what. There will be just Father and Mother to see to most times." She paused for a second to take a breath. "But the best of it is I am to go to Hatfield!"

Elizabeth's eyes were wide as she rattled off the news so fast that Robin could barely catch it all.

"I have been asked to go to the household of Lady Bryan, who hath the care of the Lady Elizabeth." Elizabeth began to slow down a little as she self-consciously used the title by which the former Princess Elizabeth was now to be called. More soberly, she explained her

*Friends in High Places*

new circumstances and began to realize the full extent of the changes in her own life.

"Most of the household have returned to court now that the Prin... now that My Lady is fallen from favour and the King hath a new Queen. She remains there with a greatly reduced staff, but I have been chosen to go, Robin. Oh, but imagine, Robin," she gasped, speaking now with more obvious joy. "I am to be with the Lady Elizabeth, and the Lady Mary is often there, and I will be there, too, with them both..." Her words ran out and she stood looking at Robin, her black curls escaping her cap as usual, and her blushing face alive with pleasure.

Robin spent the rest of the day with them, smiling and nodding and listening politely to their news and plans for the future. Master Tamar arrived home at about six and he, too, was full of excitement and pride.

"I know thee well, lad," he said, taking Robin aside, "and I have not forgotten thee, or my dear friend Thomas, God rest him. Thy work is safe on the river as long as it is required. For me, I am older now and the Mistress ails in her back and her side. The

*A Rose on the River*

country air is what we need, away from the sweat and stink of the city. As for young Elizabeth, she hath risen further than I could have dreamed, with her clever young head and her laughing ways." He glanced over at his daughter lovingly and then back to Robin.

"Fear not, young 'un, you are welcome in our new home. Changes come and time is chasing us all."

When he left for the wharf again, Robin was sad. He knew only too well that he had lost the best friends he had ever had and that there was no one in his life to replace them. He had listened to Elizabeth talk of a world in which he could never have a part: the King's displeasure, the execution of poor Queen Anne, the coming of Jane Seymour – she heard it all from the company she kept. Elizabeth would thrive, he knew, with her beauty, good humour, and quick young mind that missed nothing and remembered all.

As Robin went to sleep that night, he felt a sense of loss as great as when his Uncle Thomas had gone. His head ached with grief.

The diary entries continued, however. With little to distract him, Robin began to recognize more people, to know them by name, and to put more detail into his diary.

*October 4th, 1536*
*Conveyed Mistress Pole and young Master Pole from Whitehall to Hampton Court after their stay at Sir Nicholas Carew's house at Croydon. The rumour is that the new Queen hath made much of the Lady Mary and would reunite her with her father, the King. 'Tis said that the King and Queen traversed to Hunsdon with gifts for the Lady Mary. Methinks Elizabeth would know of this. She might well glimpse the royal party, since the household moves from Hatfield to Hunsdon oftentimes.*

— ❀ —

The winter of that year was fiercely cold and the River Thames became a platform of ice. The ceremonial procession of boats from London to Greenwich for Christmas could not take place, and the King rode with Queen Jane and his daughter Mary to St Paul's Cathedral. The frost and snow coated London in a crisp shell of white, overhanging the thatched roofs with icicle fingers reaching down into the streets. The heaps of rubbish were transformed into sparkling, snowy mounds to be jumped over and kicked by the apprentice boys as they tumbled down to the river to skate. Trapped in slabs of ice, the boats became floating shops serving mulled ale and hot chestnuts.

The sharp night frosts and the biting wind spared nothing in the streets of London. The houses seemed to huddle even closer together as the winter gales cleansed the city of disease and blew away any lingering stench of summer. Young and old found a cold companionship in the freezing days. As London and Westminster joined together on the ice to celebrate the New Year, the river traffic was at a standstill.

It was on such a bitter winter morning that Robin, idling by the barge with two other young boatmen, was surprised to hear his name being called across the river.

"Robin! Robin Smythe! Here, Robin, here!" A female voice was calling out to him, cutting through the icy mist overhanging the Thames that day.

Out of the fog surrounding the approaching figure came a hint of lavender and rose. Before

*Friends in High Places*

he saw her smiling face, Robin knew it was Elizabeth. He could not conceal his joy.

"Look out ahead!" she yelled as she skated towards him, out of control. Robin's companions caught hold of her richly cloaked arms and Robin felt the fur at her wrists and the soft leather of her gloves. The Tamars certainly had risen in the world.

"Elizabeth!" exclaimed Robin. "What brings thee here?"

"Why, thine own sweet self, Robin Smythe. Now find me some fire lest I freeze to death!"

At this, the others disappeared and the two friends were left alone. As before, Robin only sat and listened as Elizabeth chattered about her life, her adventures, and her new friends. Although she was taller and had a new air of experience about her, her manner was as lively, and her face as fresh and pretty, as it ever was.

Life at Hatfield, it seemed, was ordered and scholarly. The Lady Elizabeth had a wonderful governess named Catherine Champernowne, who was teaching her languages and other subjects. The Lady Elizabeth learned quickly, and Elizabeth Tamar was often asked to join the lessons so that they could practise conversing together.

"She hath such a pale face," remarked Elizabeth, "and her hair is as golden as the King's. She is most serious, but methinks she likes me well enough, for I can make her smile on the saddest of days."

Robin could imagine the freshness and humour that Elizabeth would bring to the sternest Latin or French lesson.

"But she is a true princess, Robin, whatever men say of her mother. She is so tall and proud. Truth to tell, I am in fear of her sometimes, for she will show her temper to us all. Methinks she would remind us of her royal blood, although she is but a child."

"Thy tongue is faster than my head, Elizabeth," interrupted Robin. "What brings thee home to London?"

"Why, Robin, didst thou not hear? The Lady Elizabeth is taken with a sore head and aching limbs. I was removed to Hunsdon with the Lady Mary and have escorted her to London, where she is reunited with her father, the King."

It was clear from what Elizabeth Tamar said that she had become a popular and trusted

*Friends in High Places*

member of the household under Lady Bryan. She had been chosen for her ability in languages, her liveliness, and her youth. Her family's lack of previous court connections also made her "safe".

Now, however, it seemed that Elizabeth Tamar, who was eight years older than the young Lady Elizabeth, had also formed an attachment to the Lady Mary. The King's elder daughter was Elizabeth Tamar's senior by nine years, but her sad and bitter life had been enriched by the new arrival's company. The two had spent many hours together while the Lady Elizabeth was busy at her music lessons, or mastering the many other skills she took to so readily.

In a little less than an hour, Robin was watching Elizabeth disappear into the winter's morning. Leaden clouds from the east blew across the river. With more snow threatening, the city folk stole back to their fires.

Robin's heart grew heavy once more. For weeks after, he would look out for Elizabeth across the river banks, imagining he saw her from afar, or heard her calling across the river. But she did not return that winter, or the next.

*A Rose on the River*

From time to time, Robin received letters from his young friend – brief, chattering letters that he would read and reread. They caused some talk among the boatmen. No one else on the river received notes carried by servants from the countryside. Sometimes, Master Tamar himself would call at the wharf to talk to Robin, or pass him a note, but Elizabeth did not return. It was the spring of 1542 before they met again.

# Chapter Six

## A Visit to the Tamars

April, 1542. Spring was returning to London, rustling through the trees that lined the quieter parts of the river, hemming its swings and curves with green lace and blossom. The King now had his much-wanted son. Prince Edward had been born in 1537, at the cost of Jane Seymour's life.

Just over two years after Queen Jane died of complications following Edward's birth, Henry married Anne of Cleves, and divorced her six months later. Now he had a new queen, the young Catherine Howard. The King's relationship with his daughters was not close, and was mostly confined to essential court occasions. He was ageing rapidly and his legs were ulcerated and painful. There was no time, it seemed, for the feelings or needs of Mary and Elizabeth.

The fortunes of the Lady Elizabeth had plummeted in the years following her mother's death. At times, Lady Bryan was forced to write to the King to beg for more money to pay for the upkeep of the household. Elizabeth Tamar's letters to Robin reflected these changed fortunes, and at times she wrote of her yearning to be back with her own mother. But she dared not upset her royal patrons, and so she led a life that was increasingly studious and restricted.

Towards the middle of the month, Robin was called into the small office on the wharf, where a servant of the Tamars awaited him.

"Mistress Tamar hath passed away, Robin." The servant blurted out the news, and Robin was speechless for a moment.

"Oh nay, not the Mistress!" he responded at last, and immediately felt ashamed of his

## A Visit to the Tamars

surprise. "I should have known. I should have enquired after her, knowing how frail and feeble she looked."

"Well, the Master said I was to come for thee at once. The young mistress hath come down from Hatfield, and she is sore upset and asking for thee."

Robin looked at the bargekeeper, who nodded in response. "Aye, go lad, if Master Tamar bids it. Get ye gone this day."

And so Robin left the river for a week or more, taking with him the clothes he stood up in and his diaries. He thought Elizabeth might be interested to see how he had kept them up over the years. Besides, a little reading might distract her.

---

Tamar House was a grand place made of brick and surrounded by pasture land, with an orchard at the south-facing end. Although it was a house filled with sadness, it was still warm and welcoming. Robin wept with Elizabeth when he heard about how Mistress Tamar had fought her illness and then died peacefully in her husband's arms.

Elizabeth had changed. She was as lovely and as friendly to Robin as ever, but he sensed a reserve in her that was not there before. She was not so eager to talk about her life as she had been. She spent time locked away in her room, scribbling letters and notes that were taken away from the house by servants. Robin put this remoteness down to the loss of her mother. It seemed she was growing up at last. Inconsolable, Master Tamar kept to his room and Robin hardly saw him during his stay.

One afternoon, when the sunshine drew the two friends out into the garden, Robin thought it might be a good time to show Elizabeth his diaries.

"Heavens, Robin, hast thou kept these diaries even now?" she gasped when he offered them to her.

"Aye," answered Robin. "I thought it might be of interest to thee, for I have logged some comings and goings these past few years."

Elizabeth began to browse politely through the diaries. Suddenly, she stopped reading and looked up sharply.

"Robin, wouldst thou fetch me a drink from within? 'Tis so very warm."

## A Visit to the Tamars

Robin did as he was asked. When he returned, Elizabeth could be seen across the garden, feverishly flicking through the pages of one of the diaries with a look of concern on her face. As she caught sight of him, the look vanished and was replaced by her familiar smile.

"Thou dost amaze me, Robin. Thou hast grown so clever with thy words and thy findings." She put the diaries down and sat back in her seat, more relaxed as she sipped her drink. "So many important folk on thy barge. Look, even Signor Chapuys, the Spanish Ambassador. Thou hast writ it all, and the times and the places. Thou hast writ it all!"

Robin smiled back at her proudly. "Indeed I have. Thou hast not been the only one sitting amongst the royal court!" He meant this as a joke, of course, but Elizabeth did not seem amused. There were other things on her mind.

"Is this thy latest volume, Robin, or hast thou more?" she enquired at last.

"There is one more," he replied, "writ just these last few months, but 'tis stowed in the barge. There was not time to fetch it away."

Elizabeth's eyes rested thoughtfully on Robin as a voice from the house called them in. The diaries were not discussed again. When it was time for Robin to return to the river, a cloud of melancholy descended over him. He feared it would be years before he and Elizabeth met again.

As he took his leave, Master Tamar surprised Robin by embracing him warmly.

"Art thou treated well on the wharf, boy?" he asked, releasing his grip on Robin's shoulders and looking at him kindly.

"Aye, thanks to thee, sir, I am fairly treated," replied Robin.

"Take care, boy," he said quietly as he turned back to the house.

"What of thee, Elizabeth?" asked Robin.

"I shall return to Hatfield for now, but I know not what the future holds." Elizabeth looked up at Robin, who now stood head and shoulders above her.

"The Lady Elizabeth hath less time for me since her brother, Prince Edward, joined the household. She truly cares for him and will hear nothing against her father, the King."

"Does she speak of her mother, Queen Anne?" ventured Robin, who rarely asked questions of this kind.

## A Visit to the Tamars

"No, not at all. Methinks she hath no memory of Queen Anne. She speaks only of her great father and how he is the kindest prince in Christendom. The Lady Mary hath told me enough of this 'kind Prince', enough to make me…" But now she stopped herself short and glanced at Robin.

"Enough to make me speak treason of the King if I have not a care!" She threw back her head and laughed. "Oh, Robin, get ye safely back to the river, lest both our heads be on the block!"

Robin laughed, too, and waved farewell as he mounted the docile horse that Master Tamar had provided to carry him back to the outskirts of the city.

In less than an hour, he was back at the wharf, already picking over his time with the Tamars, when one of the boat boys stuck his tousled head out the boathouse doorway and called to him.

"Robin, thou art missed from here. I have searched for thee these last three days."

"What's amiss, Luke?" asked Robin.

"Why, 'tis that book. The one ye write in, Robin, wi' the black calf cover."

Robin looked up sharply. Luke was speaking of the diary he had left on the barge.

"Well, 'tis torn and covered in mud and muck. Young Nick found it nigh on low tide. Methinks it dropped o'erboard somewise, but truth to tell 'tis ruined, Robin, and all the pages missing."

# Chapter Seven

## Return of the Fool

May, 1542. The May blossom that had welcomed Queen Anne Boleyn to the throne, then witnessed her execution on Tower Green just a few years later, bloomed once more in the gardens of Hampton Court and on the quiet reaches of the river. Robin sat on the barge as it made its return to Greenwich, trying to relax before the busy river traffic again demanded his whole attention.

He was disturbed by the events of the last few weeks. There was his visit to the Tamars and the loss of his diary. Now, this very morning, as he loaded passengers onto the barge, he had seen a group of strolling players. Among them, he was sure he had caught a glimpse of scarlet and gold.

That glimpse had taken him back many years, to the day he first came to the wharf and was robbed. A stranger dressed as a Fool had helped him that day. The same Fool, Robin suspected, who had later been punished for speaking ill of Anne Boleyn. He had no proof that it was the same person who had called himself the King's Fool, but the flash of red and yellow had made him turn and stare.

As Robin stepped from the barge to take a closer look, a crowd had formed around the players, who began to sing and dance. It *was* the Fool! He was dressed almost exactly as before, although this time the stick in his hand had a grotesque man's head on it, fashioned with a beard and a crown not unlike that of King Henry himself. Despite the passing of several years, the Fool was able to tumble and somersault as well as ever and Robin stole a moment to watch. As he was standing there, the Fool came leaping towards

*Return of the Fool*

him and shoved him to one side, almost knocking him over.

"Look out!" Robin gasped. The Fool steadied Robin with one hand and with the other swiftly passed him a scrap of paper.

"Get thee gone!" he hissed at Robin. Then, in an instant, he was gone himself.

Robin jumped back on the barge, keeping the paper in his pocket until they were midstream and everyone was settled for the journey up to Hampton. When at last he opened it, he was amazed to find a message from Elizabeth Tamar.

"Help me, Robin!" it read. "Come to the house tonight. Elizabeth."

Robin's curiosity and sense of unease reached fever pitch by the early afternoon. The days on the river had grown longer as the hours of daylight increased, and Robin finally had to make an excuse to leave the barge. He hurried across the city and was out in the countryside by nightfall, a dangerous time to be travelling alone. It was very late when he arrived at Tamar House, but Robin's relief at arriving safely was soon forgotten. Was the message truly from Elizabeth, or was it all some mistake?

*A Rose on the River*

He need not have worried for, at the sight of his tall figure approaching the house, Elizabeth herself opened the heavy oak door and ran out to meet him.

She said no word of greeting, but pulled him inside and shut the door silently behind him. In a small upstairs room, she handed him a mug of ale. Still she did not speak.

"Pray, Elizabeth, what game is this?" asked Robin, setting aside the mug, although his throat ached with thirst.

"No game, Robin, though I wish it were with all my heart." Elizabeth seated herself beside Robin at a small wooden table and he knew that she was wordlessly urging him to drink. It was clear that the business of the night was not finished.

"My father is gone from the house, Robin, visiting with my aunt near Hever, but I am not alone here. I have a guest whose life is in great danger and I need thy help."

Robin searched her anxious face and pressed her to tell more.

"I cannot tell thee the name of my guest, but thou must know that she is most high in the land and that there are those who would rid the country of her presence. We have escaped from Hatfield this day in great haste, but will shortly be missed and searched for." Elizabeth was becoming greatly agitated and her eyes darted from the casement to the door, rarely making contact with Robin's.

"What shall I do to help thee?" asked Robin. His mind teemed with questions, but he sensed Elizabeth's urgency and the need for immediate escape.

"We are in want of a boat, Robin. We must get across the city and out onto the river, lest we are both caught and put to death this night!"

A plan was quickly made. Robin and the two young women would travel in Master Tamar's carriage back to London. There, Robin would secure a boat from the wharf and carry them safely downriver to the estuary, where a fishing boat from Cornwall was to meet them. From there they would make their escape to St Mawes Castle in Cornwall and await the actions of the King.

In view of the strange events of the day, this made sense to Robin. He knew the Tamar family had land and contacts in Cornwall and that King Henry himself had built a castle at

St Mawes. He trusted Elizabeth and wished to show it, so he asked no more questions. Nor did he speak or stare at the young woman with Elizabeth as he helped them both into the carriage and they jolted off down the rutted lane towards London.

Despite the roughness of the road and the darkness of the night, the journey went quickly. All was silent but for the wooden wheels straining and creaking on the stony road. Robin was unfamiliar with carriage driving and his hands were soon stiff with tension on the leather reins. Fortunately, the horse was a quiet beast who tolerated Robin's inexperience well for most of the journey.

They stabled the horse at an inn near the wharf and walked quickly in the direction of the river. Still they did not utter a word. The streets were scattered with homeless figures sleeping in huddles against the buildings. Stray dogs, cats, and rats scurried and squeaked underfoot. It was a frightening place to be at night, and Robin was unsure of getting to a boat without being seen.

"Elizabeth!" he whispered, taking her arm. "Stop a moment. We must talk about this!"

*Return of the Fool*

She would not stop, but pulled the hood of her cloak over her head like her companion. "No time to rest, Robin," she told him, her words muffled by the heavy cloth. "We must make haste if we are to catch the tide."

When at last they reached the wharf, the boathouses were locked securely for the night and those boats still on the river were manned as always.

"We are lost, then," said a soft, clear voice to Robin.

It was the first time Elizabeth's companion had spoken, and now Robin turned to look at her. The moonlight showed him that she was very young. He had thought her much older from her height and slim figure. Her pale face and frank eyes looked directly at him, and she spoke with confidence and calm. Robin knew immediately who she was. He did not have to look for the auburn hair or the famous long white fingers, now gloved against the cold. She had come from Hatfield, of course. It was the King's daughter, the Lady Elizabeth.

Robin looked at the two Elizabeths, whose lives so unaccountably seemed to depend upon him. Suddenly, the answer came to him.

*A Rose on the River*

"I have an idea," he said excitedly. "'Twill mean parting company, but not for long, and I fear 'tis the only way."

The soft voice of the royal lady spoke again. "Tell us, Robin. We are in danger while we stand this ground."

Robin turned to Elizabeth Tamar. "If thou wouldst remain behind, I might take our companion down to the boathouse. I will say to the keeper that 'tis thee and we are in urgent need of a boat this night."

"Dost thou not know, Robin, who this is? Wouldst thou disguise the Lady Elizabeth as Elizabeth Tamar, who is twice her age?"

"Aye, Elizabeth. Look, she is as tall as thee and thou, too, art known to have an angel's face. In this light she would pass, I am certain." Warming to his theme, Robin continued as both girls listened attentively. "'Tis only the hair colouring that might give it away, and a bit of soot from the fire in the yard would meet that need. Elizabeth, I shall meet thee downriver at Tamar's Landing. Go now and await us there!"

The plan was soon put into action. The boathouse keeper, woken from his sleep, was too muddled and full of the night's ale to argue with Robin. Questioned later, his story was simply put. "All I saw was young Master Robin and young Mistress Tamar, wrapped up against the night, with a tale of how her father was ill down at Hever. 'Tis all I heard or saw in the dark hours of the night."

Meanwhile, Elizabeth Tamar scurried alone into the night. Beyond the outskirts of the wharf buildings, she slipped into the shadows and waited before silently retracing her steps, glancing frequently over her shoulder to check that she was not followed.

Just as she neared the boathouse, a tall shadowy figure stepped out in front of her, and another appeared behind him. She gasped. Two foreign-looking gentlemen with coal black beards and dark, glittering eyes prevented her from going any further. They were both dressed in doublets and hose of rich velvet, though the colours were lost to the night. Around them they pulled cloaks of rich damask, and gold glowed dully at their ears and on their fingers.

They, too, glanced nervously around them, before beginning to speak, quickly and quietly.

If Robin had heard them, he would not have been surprised to discover that their words were not English, and they were full of hate.

# Chapter Eight

## Away into the Night

Robin, alone with the daughter of the King of England – a possible heir to the throne, despite her mother's misfortunes – fixed his mind on escape and tried to put all disbelief and fear behind him. Like the skilful sailor he was, Robin eased the small boat down the muddy wharf into the river, then held it steady so that the Lady Elizabeth could climb safely aboard.

Unused to the indignities of black river mud and damp, floating timbers, she struggled to maintain her balance. Her tiny feet were laced into soft leather shoes never meant to encounter bilge water. Her dress, soft as down to the touch, dragged a heavy trail of thick river muck after it and pulled on her slim shoulders as if it would break them. Not once did she complain or cry out in alarm. Not once, as the unsteady boat threatened to tip the two of them into the inky water, did she tremble or betray her fear.

When they were both settled at last in the boat, Robin pulled on the oars and the small vessel began the short journey downriver to Tamar's Landing. The river was quiet – so still that it seemed to hold its breath lest the royal passenger be harmed. But Robin feared nothing now. He was in his element on the river. He was confident that he could ferry her safely, for he knew every twist and turn and inlet on the Thames, every mood and manner of the river's flow.

"Where is the landing at which Elizabeth waits?" asked the Lady Elizabeth, raising her head so that the moon shone on her features. A speck of soot had fallen from her auburn hair and settled on her cheek.

*Away into the Night*

"We are almost there now, My Lady," whispered Robin.

Suddenly, he was filled with dread. What if Elizabeth had not reached the landing safely? Was he wrong to have sent her off alone in the streets of London at night? He was tortured for the rest of the journey until at last he saw the outline of her body pressed up against the stone steps by the river.

"She is there!" he gasped thankfully, and he saw his passenger smile with relief.

Turning back to concentrate on his task, Robin rowed the boat as near to the steps as he could manage and waited, expecting Elizabeth to descend and climb into the boat. But she was suddenly nowhere to be seen.

"Elizabeth," he called out, as loudly as he dared. There was no reply.

"What's amiss?" the Lady Elizabeth enquired, slightly alarmed.

"Elizabeth, what ails thee? Where art thou?" Robin called again.

An anxious minute passed. At last he tied the boat loosely to an iron ring above the steps and climbed out to look for Elizabeth. As he reached the top of the short flight of stairs leading up from the water, there was a rapid flurry of movement. Two men leaped swiftly out of the darkness and set upon him, knocking his feet from under him. Robin's head met the stone steps with a sickening crunch. Stunned, he struggled briefly and then lay still.

Seeing that Robin was no longer able to stand, the two men raced down the steps to the river. As one laid hold of the rope and began pulling the drifting boat towards him, the other slid his hand under his cloak and drew out a dagger with a long, slender blade.

Inside the boat, the Lady Elizabeth had the sense to remain seated and was herself fumbling in a velvet purse strapped around her waist. Above her, Robin lay dazed but no longer unconscious. The stone steps bit into his back, but he dared not move before he had taken the measure of what was happening. There was a rapidly narrowing stretch of black river between the steps and the boat's helpless young passenger, but as yet she was showing no signs of panic.

Briefly, Robin turned his head away from the scene on the river. As he did so, the smell of lavender and rose filled his nostrils.

Elizabeth! He looked up to see her standing over him. Had she come again out of the night to save his life?

She moved, and suddenly he was struggling to make sense of a truly nightmarish sight. His childhood friend was raising her arm from her side and bringing it down upon his head! In her hand was a moss-covered stone from the river bank. Her eyes said it all – she meant to kill him!

Leaving Robin for dead, Elizabeth ran away into the blackness of the street. Waiting for her at the end of an alley was a covered goods wagon. She ran as fast as she could towards it, holding her skirts up away from her ankles with both hands and shouting, "Onwards, move forward! 'Tis I!"

As she called, the wagon stirred into movement, slowly at first. Just as Elizabeth reached it, the canvas curtains at the back parted and an arm appeared between them.

Stretching out, it grasped Elizabeth, pulling her up and onto the cart. Then both arm and girl disappeared into the wagon, but not before the breaking dawn light had exposed a flash of scarlet and gold on its sleeve.

Back at the river steps, the Lady Elizabeth drew from her purse a small blade and began to cut through the rope that joined the boat to the frantic assassins. Behind them, Robin fought against the throbbing pain from the gash in his head and tried to find focus enough to stand.

The men were fumbling badly, hindered by their voluminous cloaks and the treacherous slime that clung to the stone, denying them a sure footing on the steps. Then, as the Lady Elizabeth at last sliced through the rope and freed herself, the taller of the two men pointed a vicious finger at her and shouted in heavily accented English. "A curse on thee, Elizabeth, misbegotten daughter of a witch!"

For the first time, Robin saw her shudder and turn her face away in fear. Before the men could turn back up the steps, he dragged himself to the edge and half-fell, half-dived into the river. A few swift, spluttering strokes reunited him with the boat, now moving slowly away on the current. Fear and determination aided him as he laid hold of the gunwale and pulled himself on board. Dripping foul river water, he grabbed quickly at the oars and regained control of the boat. He knew he must row as fast as he could, for soon the river's inhabitants would appear to begin their morning rituals. And he must ignore the fact that he had not eaten or rested for many hours and his clothes were soaked and filthy.

"Where might I convey thee, My Lady?" he croaked, feeling foolish at the thought of how he must appear to his royal passenger.

The Lady Elizabeth's face was sad as she replied quietly. "Whom can we trust? We know not who tried to kill us this night, Robin. There is no safe place in London for a King's daughter whom the people wish to see dead."

"'Tis not the people, My Lady. Those men are from Spain. I have carried them before on the barge, and I can prove how they have travelled the river and with whom they are friends, for 'tis all in my di…"

Robin stopped himself. He remembered that it was all logged in the diary that had been torn and thrown in the river while he was with the Tamars. So now it made sense. Elizabeth Tamar was involved in a conspiracy to kidnap, and perhaps even murder, the Lady Elizabeth. She had been aware of the plot for a long time and knew that the diary might link her and others to the Spaniards on the river.

It must be so, for Elizabeth Tamar was the only one who knew about the diary. Robin had tried hard to put it out of his mind, but he saw now that it was too much of a coincidence that the diary should be destroyed accidentally that week, of all weeks. Now, as he remembered the scent of lavender and rose, and Elizabeth's lovely face above him, he knew that she was guilty of this terrible crime.

# Chapter Nine

## Dawn on the River

The grey dawn lifted the cover that had enabled Robin and his passenger to row in safety on the river. He dared not think about the Spaniards' next move, or with whom they were in league. If nothing else, Robin's fellow river workers would be on the lookout for him and Elizabeth Tamar, once the boatkeeper had gathered his wits and thought through the events of the past night.

"My Lady, we should go to the King!" Robin pleaded again.

The Lady Elizabeth shook her head. "The King is away at sport," she replied. Robin guessed that this was probably not true. He tried to read the thoughts of his passenger, and imagined that she was remembering her mother's fate at the hands of her father. Was she willing to risk the King's involvement in this? She would not want to believe that the father she loved so well, yet saw so little, might wish her harm. But perhaps it was difficult to trust the King, even if you were his daughter.

Robin was trembling as the morning river mists chilled the soaking clothes on his back and pains of hunger gnawed at his stomach. How was it that this pampered royal child, not yet nine years old, could sit so calmly and sensibly when she had been close to death and might yet be hunted like an animal?

Not for the first time, Robin felt ashamed of his weakness, but he knew that if he did not get dry clothes and food in his stomach he would take a fever and be of no further use to the Lady Elizabeth.

He decided to double back along the river. The men who had attacked them would have left the scene by now. They had probably taken

*Dawn on the River*

horses to ride the length of the river bank in search of the pair. Hugging the left bank, which was lined with warehouses and buildings and inaccessible from the street, Robin forced his failing arms to pull the boat back upriver to the wharf. The neighbourhood was stirring into activity. As they approached, Robin could hear the boatkeeper talking to Luke and some other barge boys.

"Aye, last night he came. Some trouble with young Mistress Tamar and her father, I believe. He hath taken a boat and I doubt we shall see him this day."

Robin tied the boat up quickly and, as the men talked on the wharf, he climbed up a set of narrow steps at the back of the boathouse. The Lady Elizabeth, agile and strong, despite her age, followed silently. Bending low, Robin motioned to her to wait while he stole into his sleeping quarters and quickly found dry clothes. His dripping jerkin was lying on the floor when the boatkeeper entered and caught Robin struggling into a clean shirt.

"Why, Robin, 'tis thee! What game is this to wake me from my sleep? Methinks..." The old boatkeeper stopped, for he had caught sight of another figure, cloaked but clearly young and female, entering the room.

"Mistress Tamar, what ails thy father?" asked the boatkeeper.

The Lady Elizabeth kept her head down and Robin answered quickly.

"Good sir, forgive us, but Mistress Tamar cannot speak for grief."

"Not dead?" gasped the boatkeeper.

"Nay, nay, not dead, but poorly, and we must away to the house." Robin searched for coins among his belongings and in an instant he and his companion were gone.

At the inn they had briefly visited the night before, they found the horse and carriage still stabled. Robin bought bread and cheese from the innkeeper and they headed north out of London. About two miles along the road, Robin turned to the Lady Elizabeth and saw that she, too, was exhausted. He pulled the carriage off the road and, in the shelter of a small grove of trees, he tied up the horse and prepared to rest.

It was mid-afternoon before Robin stirred again. He looked over at the sun glinting gold and red on his sleeping companion's head and shuddered when he thought of all the dangers that might still overtake them on the road. He thanked God that they were safe so far. Robin's instinct told him to make for Tamar House, but, if Elizabeth was there, it would mean renewed danger. Once again, he tried to shut his mind to the thought of Elizabeth Tamar, his dear, dear friend. She had turned against him and tricked him. Once, she had saved his life. Last night, it seemed she was willing to take that life away.

She would have known what to do now, thought Robin. He felt ashamed that he was too dull and tired to come up with an ingenious plan to save his youthful charge. And so, when the Lady Elizabeth herself proposed a solution, he was only too happy to listen.

"Robin, we must make for Hatfield. Lady Bryan and Kate Champernowne would not harm me, for they have had their chance a hundred times over. That was why Elizabeth lured me away from there down to London."

The girl was refreshed now and her eyes flashed with carefully contained anger. "My sweet friend Elizabeth did not take us away from danger. She led us into it!" But that glint of anger was soon followed by tears as she realized the extent of the deception.

Robin listened as the Lady Elizabeth put her thoughts into words. Now, his friend's mysterious duplicity began at last to make a chilling sense.

"Elizabeth hath spent so much time with our sister, the Lady Mary, and we have been warned there might be plots against us, born of sympathy for our sister's cause."

Once again, Robin noticed how she sometimes used the royal plural when referring to herself. It seemed odd in one so young. "But, My Lady, why should anyone plot against thee?" he asked her.

"The Spanish would put a Catholic queen on the throne again. They are much grieved for the manner in which Queen Catherine of Aragon was used, and Mary, too. For myself, I bear no malice towards her, for I do believe her to be innocent of such plotting, or of any desire to foster it in others. We have heard our sister say that our sweet brother Edward is not strong and that he may not live long, but he is the son of our father, the King, and rightful heir to the throne."

Robin was amazed that this young girl should know so much of affairs of state. He began to realize that, in some ways, she was as alone in the world as he was. Robin had never dreamed that he would feel sorry for a king's daughter.

The danger was not over, however, and so, as the Lady Elizabeth talked, Robin set the wheels in motion and turned the horse towards Hatfield. It was a long way and, despite the urgency they both felt, they stopped several times on the journey. They were not alone on the road. They passed merchants travelling to the city and farmers herding sheep and cows to market. Fortunately, no one gave them a second glance.

"Pray, My Lady, would not Lady Bryan and thy servants raise the alarm?" asked Robin, for he had quite expected to see men on the road in search of a lost royal lady.

"Nay, for Elizabeth was cunning and said that she would escort us to Hunsdon to rest for the night. The household was happy to see us gone, for our brother Edward was coughing badly again these two days past and they were afeared lest we also fall ill," she explained.

"Just thee and Mistress Tamar on the road alone, My Lady?" he persisted.

"Aye, Robin. The household was taken ill with the cough. Even my dear Kate. Now forward, boy, and keep thy silence!" The Lady Elizabeth had talked enough it seemed.

The road led them through part of the Ashridge estate, a treasury of wild flowers and trees stretching over the chalk downland. After the years Robin had spent on the river, the sight of a fallow deer grazing among ash and beech groves filled him with a sense of freedom and joy in his escape from the city.

Robin had not spoken for a while – he did not want to risk another curt rebuff – and it was his companion who spoke first this time.

"Robin, art thou sure of this road? 'Tis a long way from Hatfield, we venture."

No, Robin was not sure they were on the right road. He had become absorbed in the beauty of his surroundings, and the quietness of the road had lulled his worries about being seen or even captured. He had rashly allowed himself to relax for the first time in hours.

Robin stopped the carriage and looked towards the east. In the distance, the ancient

*Dawn on the River*

Hatfield oaks and horse chestnuts could just be seen.

"I am turning eastwards, My Lady. See, methinks yon oaks belong to Hatfield Forest!" said Robin, extending his finger to show her the way.

"Indeed, Robin," she replied haughtily. "We do see the forest."

# Chapter Ten

## Secret Messages

Also making its way north, having rested for a few hours at Tamar House, was a covered goods wagon last seen near the Thames river bank. At the front of the wagon sat two Spanish acrobats, both dressed in vibrant colours. They had spent their lives travelling around Europe with different groups of performers and play actors, and now they were masters of their art.

The first was quite small in stature, but his shoulders were thickset and muscular. His hair was black, like jet, and curly. It twisted around his ears and tumbled across his brow. He was probably about twenty-five years old, but his skin was as lined and leathery as that of a man twice his age. His days and many of his nights were spent out in the open, in the sun, wind, and rain.

His friend, who held the reins of the pony that pulled them along the dusty road, was equally broad in the shoulders, but his body was otherwise long and lean. He had a gold earring in his left ear. His other ear was hidden by long straight hair, tied back in a neat braid that reached below his shoulders. His dark eyes never wavered from the road, and the only sound he made was an occasional word of encouragement to the pony.

The driver's greatest skill was in the juggling of balls, batons, or hoops while balanced on another man's shoulders, or a narrow piece of rope. He amazed the crowds by eating fire, swallowing the billowing amber flames and sending up coils of black smoke. He would then walk on his hands or somersault across the floor as the audience cheered and clapped.

*A Rose on the River*

The third member of their act sat inside the wagon opposite Elizabeth Tamar. She was dark-haired like her companion, but there the resemblance ended. Where Elizabeth had the soft, peachy skin of a life lived largely indoors, in every comfort, this young woman had the deeply bronzed skin of a sunnier climate.

They were sitting together, heads bent forward, deep in conversation, when a cry from behind brought the wagon to a halt.

As the dust cloud subsided, a youth on horseback could be seen, his mount panting slightly from its exertions. Without speaking, the Fool, still dressed in his trademark scarlet and gold, jumped from his lookout position at the rear of the wagon. He was handed a note written in Spanish, which he passed to Elizabeth. She read it quickly, then turned in obvious alarm to her fellow travellers, and began to speak in Spanish.

"In English, if you please!" interrupted the Fool. "I am but a fool, as ye know well enough."

"The plan hath failed! It seems that, after we left, those halfwits failed to land their precious catch. She hath escaped, they know not where!"

*Secret Messages*

As Elizabeth spoke, she reviewed the events of the previous night and was shocked anew by her own part in them. The last thing she had wanted was for Robin to be hurt. She had used him badly in this plot to kidnap the Lady Elizabeth, and she knew that such a breach of trust would break their friendship forever. Elizabeth had convinced herself that, however painful the loss of Robin's love would be, it was a small sacrifice for the future of England and Wales.

She had listened for months to the sad story of the Lady Mary, and how her mother, Catherine of Aragon, had been so foully treated by the King. The young women had discussed their shared Catholic faith and how King Henry had acted against the Pope and betrayed all true believers.

The Lady Mary had also spoken harshly of Queen Anne, the mother of her sister Elizabeth. "That upstart Nan Bullen hath treated us with contempt and we despise her for it! The day my dear mother died, Queen Anne rejoiced and the King, our father, dressed in gaudy yellow and carried Elizabeth shoulder high for all the court to see!"

Slowly, Elizabeth Tamar's loyalty had turned away from her namesake, whose Protestant sympathies were an open secret. When whispers reached her, through like-minded friends, of a desperate plan to kidnap the young Lady Elizabeth, and thus remove her from the line of succession, she was at first horrified. Her position in the royal household and her knowledge of Spanish made her a valuable ally, however, and the pressure on her to join the conspiracy was constant. In the end, it was irresistible.

The Fool and the players were easily involved. Under cover of entertaining the royal children, they had often passed messages between Catholic sympathizers at court and the Lady Mary's household.

Now the dangerous plan had failed, largely thanks to the bungling of the Spanish nobles entrusted with the river abduction. Rather than face the wrath of the King, they were already fleeing back to their homeland. Elizabeth's thoughts flew at once to her royal patron. Mary had known nothing of this foolhardy scheme, but would she be blamed for what her supporters had so badly mismanaged?

*Secret Messages*

"A warning must be sent to the Lady Mary at once!" snapped Elizabeth. The cipher she used was well known and involved nothing more than a simple reversal of the alphabet, but Elizabeth had no time to invent anything else. The coded message carried to the Lady Mary read:

"Ulitrev fh, Ozwb. Z kozm gl gzpv Vorazyvgs szgs uzrovw. Ollp gl gsbhvou."

The Fool spoke next and his words rang with an authority that calmed the others and decided the next move. "We must away to Scotland with all possible speed. The King hath too much on his royal mind at present to concern himself overmuch with the tale of a barge boy. With luck, we might all escape with our heads."

Elizabeth doubted his words and said so. "King Henry dare not ignore an attempt by the Spanish on his daughter's life!"

At this, the Spanish girl spoke for the first time since the wagon had stopped. Her English was poor, but her meaning was clear. "This King, he hath too much pain in the legs and too much trouble in the heart. He hath been betrayed and made the fool by another young queen. He will not want a fight with Chapuys at this time!"

The truth of these words hit home at once. The girl was right!

And so the covered wagon resumed its journey. Its destination was many days' ride ahead in Scotland, where Elizabeth Tamar and her friends would find allies and sympathizers with the Catholic cause. But, as the pony negotiated the deep holes and ruts in the road, Elizabeth's emotions were in turmoil. The King's soldiers could be awaiting them at any turn, and she might not escape with her life, but one thing was certain: she could not return to her beloved father and she would never see Robin again. For all she knew, she had killed him herself with that blow to the head.

First I save him and then I murder him! she thought, then laughed out loud.

"What amuses thee, Elizabeth?" enquired the Spanish girl.

"Nothing," replied Elizabeth, turning her head away. "Nothing amuses me." Her eyes burned with tears.

# Chapter Eleven

## Old Friends

The sky above Hatfield Forest and the surrounding countryside grew darker. In the distance, grey clouds hung heavily over the woodlands, threatening a storm.

"Methinks we should find shelter for the night, My Lady," said Robin. "'Tis black as night o'er yon!"

He urged the tired horse forward, and the little carriage rattled on eastwards, bearing its royal passenger to the unseen safety of Hatfield House. Robin had lived in fear of thunder and lightning since that terrible night on the river when he had been tossed overboard and his dear Uncle Thomas had been lost. Images of the raging river bursting its banks, and swallowing up the little boats like some demented sea serpent, were always with him when the sky grew stormy. He tightened his hold on the reins and called to the horse to quicken its pace once more.

The Lady Elizabeth pulled her cloak closer around her in anticipation of the rain to come. "'Tis clear we are miles from Hatfield even now!" she snapped, without troubling to hide her irritation, as the first drops began to fall. "Make for the trees!"

Robin did as he was instructed, awkwardly turning horse and carriage towards a wooded area nearby. Behind the trees, the edge of a wide stretch of marshland was hidden by the gathering dusk.

Every few minutes, Robin glanced up at the gloomy sky, then from the sky to the woodland ahead. He had quickly learned how to handle the carriage, but he was not yet experienced enough to take his eye off the path ahead for more than a few seconds.

It was the dipping of the horse's neck and a neigh of surprise that jolted Robin's attention to the ground beneath them. The hard, stony turf had given way to marshland, with no warning. Within seconds, horse and carriage were in serious trouble. The vehicle lurched from left to right as the poor animal struggled in increasing panic. The reeds and grasses of the marsh gave no indication of the depth of water below the surface.

Instinctively, the Lady Elizabeth clutched at Robin's arm, her pale face wide-eyed with fear. The wooden wheels creaked to a halt. There was a splintering noise of wood against metal. Pulling back its lips to expose yellow teeth and a huge lolling tongue, the horse cried out again in terror.

Almost simultaneously, Robin and his royal charge began to shriek. "Help! Help! Anyone help us, please!"

There was no sight or sound of anyone across the marsh. Robin had no idea what to do. If they climbed out of the carriage, they would sink to their waists at the very least. If they stayed where they were, they would be pulled down with the carriage.

A long and anxious minute passed before the Lady Elizabeth took charge.

"Cut the horse free!" she commanded, passing Robin the little knife with which she had severed the rope and saved her life on the boat. Freed of the weight of the carriage, the horse floundered forward into the marsh, where the water was deeper and the marsh more treacherous than ever. The Lady Elizabeth prepared to climb over the side of the carriage.

"Stop, My Lady!" yelled Robin. "Thou wilt sink like a stone!" Robin was thinking more clearly now. "I shall hold the carriage steady and thou must climb up the side and onto the roof. I shall follow thee!"

The girl ripped her hampering velvet cloak from her shoulders and climbed onto the roof as swiftly as if she did such a thing every day.

"Now thee, Robin. Make haste, I beseech thee!" She leaned on one side of the carriage to maintain its balance as he clambered up to join her on the roof. Now, in this moment of danger, they were equals at last.

"Oh, Robin... the horse!" The Lady Elizabeth pointed out into the marsh, where the head of the ill-fated animal was now almost completely

*Old Friends*

submerged. The storm clouds hung motionless overhead, spectators at a grisly scene.

"Look away!" shouted Robin, but not before both of them had witnessed the awful end of a trusted friend.

"Keep still, but shout!" instructed Robin.

And so they did, and in time fate willed that their lives should again be spared. A bent figure emerged from the thickly knitted hedgerows and hurried, as best he could, towards them. It was a grey-haired old man who had answered them.

"Aye, aye, I be coming, hold on there!"

As he neared the carriage, he stopped and made a rapid assessment of the situation. To Robin's dismay, he then turned and went back into the hedgerow. The frightened pair barely had time to glance at each other, however, before the man reappeared.

"He's dragging something from the hedge!" shouted Robin.

They watched as the man struggled with a kind of raft made of lengths of beech or hazel strapped together with reeds. The carriage had sunk so much that they were now afraid to make any movement or noise, and they sat silently as their saviour made tantalizingly slow progress across the marsh.

At last, the old man hauled himself onto the raft. With a long pole, he began to lever his way towards them. Robin fixed his eyes on the weathered face as it came nearer and found, to his confusion, that the features seemed familiar to him.

"Lower thyselves as slow as thou might, young 'uns," shouted the man, steadying the raft until it was almost alongside the carriage. He stretched the pole out to them and Robin leaned nervously over to grasp it. As he did so, he heard a sharp intake of breath.

"Pray, boy…" The old man faltered and stared in disbelief. "Why, Robin, 'tis thee!"

Robin gasped, too. His heart pounded furiously, for he was looking down into the face of Thomas Smythe!

# Chapter Twelve

## Letters from Friends

Hatfield House, with its arched windows and safe, sturdy bricks, welcomed the Lady Elizabeth and her two companions with relief. The household, now recovering from the illness that had so alarmed Lady Bryan, had received no word of her and was worried.

During the days that followed, messages passed between Hatfield and the palace at Whitehall. Soon, a well-rested Lady Elizabeth set off to visit the court and Thomas and Robin were left to pick up the pieces of their lives.

*A Rose on the River*

Thomas was overjoyed to have been reunited with Robin, and he was far more concerned with the boy and his life and welfare than his unlikely involvement with the Lady Elizabeth. It seemed that, though the royal household was deeply indebted to Robin, it did not want to make too much of the incident that had brought him there. He and Thomas were soon transported back to London without ceremony.

In the late summer of that same year of 1542, a letter arrived at the wharf, addressed to Robin and carried by one of Master Tamar's servants. Robin read it hastily and went to make arrangements to travel to Tamar House that evening, as requested in the letter.

He remembered his last visit only too well, and it was with some sense of dread that he arrived at the house. An anxious-looking servant took Robin immediately into the Master's chamber, where bread and pease pudding awaited him.

Master Tamar was sitting in a high-backed chair before a smoking log fire. He looked up when Robin entered and motioned him to sit in a chair opposite his own.

"Sit down, Robin, and break thy fast." Master Tamar looked pitifully sad as he spoke. In his hand was a large piece of paper covered in the familiar hand of Elizabeth Tamar.

Robin thanked him and ate silently, waiting for his old friend and employer to speak when he was ready.

"My heart is full of sorrow this day, Robin," he began. "Sorrow and shame. She hath been the apple of my eye. Since the day she was born, the Mistress and I…"

Master Tamar sighed and gazed into the fire. When he spoke again, he looked directly at Robin for the first time since he arrived.

"She hath told it all in this letter… Her shame and wickedness. She feared she killed thee, Robin, and her heart is heavy for that."

"Where is Elizabeth?" asked Robin, his mind full of her sweet, soft face and the scent of lavender and rose.

"Hundreds of miles from this place, boy. They have fled to Scotland, lest they be caught and tried – as right they should be for such wicked deeds against the King's daughter!"

Robin and Master Tamar sat together talking many hours into the night. Elizabeth's

## A Rose on the River

letter to her beloved father had told him everything frankly. She had made it clear that she might never be able to return to England or see him again.

"She wants me to search for thee and, if thou livest, beseech thee to take her place in this house," explained the old man tearfully. "She says that thou must be my heir, since she is not worthy of my love. Oh, Robin, thou knowest I love the girl more than the world! I should love her no matter what wickedness she undertook!"

"And I, too!" whispered Robin, so faintly that his words were lost in the heavy air of that smoky chamber.

And so it was that Robin left his life on the River Thames and came to Tamar House. He had nothing to bring with him but his honesty, his faithfulness, and the good news about Thomas, which he had kept as a welcome surprise for Master Tamar.

The two old men wept when they were reunited, and wrapped their arms about each other like the long-lost friends they were. The house, which had once been full of the feminine scents of Elizabeth and her mother,

*Letters from Friends*

was now the home of three male companions. Lavender and rose gave way to the aroma of smoke and ale.

—— ❀ ——

In July, 1544, the silence that had fallen over those dangerous hours shared by Robin and the Lady Elizabeth was suddenly broken. Robin was in the stables at Tamar House when the unexpected clatter of horses' hoofs made him stop what he was doing and go to take a look.

Out in the cobbled yard, two riders wearing the King's livery came to a halt before him and one shouted, "Message from the Lady Elizabeth Tudor for Robin Smythe!"

All the occupants and workers at the house gathered in the yard to gaze at the two men on horseback, both clad in tunics embroidered with the Tudor Rose.

"'Tis I," said Robin and took the letter from them. He read the contents swiftly and then nodded to the men. "Wait, please. I would write an answer!"

He carried the letter into the house, where Thomas and Master Tamar awaited him, their very different faces showing a comically similar mix of curiosity and anxiety.

"What's amiss?" asked Thomas.

Robin sat them down and read aloud the message he had received.

*Hatfield House*
*July, 1544*

*To my humble servant, Robin, who hath saved the life of this Lady and hath most obediently kept secret on the matter. Robin, we are most happy on this day, for we have survived the blows of our enemies thus far.*

*Our seclusion at Hatfield is to end, and we are to return to court by the good will of our dear new Queen Catherine Parr. It is most glorious that our dear father, the King, hath granted permission for this Lady and her brother, Prince Edward, to join the Queen. We are to rest together as a family and past sadness betwixt our royal sister and ourself shall be forgotten. We pray that, before we quit this place, thou shalt visit with ourself and Lady Bryan.*

*It is also our wish that, one day, thou shalt come to court and present thyself to Their Gracious Majesties, King Henry and Queen Catherine.*

*Elizabeth*

The visit to Hatfield did take place within the following month, and the journey this time was leisurely and peaceful. The forest was splendid as the coming autumn gilded the leaves of the ancient woodland and lent the skies clarity and radiance.

Robin had become a man. Despite his humble beginnings, he had touched the lives of the royal Tudors. He had faced great danger and been party to events that might have changed history. But Robin did not dwell on such matters. He always turned his face to the future, having learned from the past.

At Hatfield he was treated with an informal respect and gratitude. During his last visit, it had been made clear to him that it would benefit no one if the details of the plot against the Lady Elizabeth were to be made public. Discretion was a quality highly valued in life at court.

*A Rose on the River*

Robin was greeted warmly by Lady Bryan, Catherine Champernowne, and the Lady Elizabeth herself, who was far more talkative and amusing than Robin remembered her. She played and sang for him and they feasted on roast swan and quails' eggs. Used to simpler fare, Robin tasted all the delights the court had to offer: meats and fish of many kinds, syllabubs and sweetmeats.

Robin was overwhelmed and the Lady Elizabeth was obviously delighted with him, but the words that passed between them when they parted remain a secret to this day.

The Lady Elizabeth did go back to the court of Henry VIII, and there she spent one of the happiest times of her life. Queen Catherine Parr was the nearest to a mother she had known and something resembling a real family was created around her, for a few short years at least. The future remained uncertain for the young Lady Elizabeth, but in 1545 her life was at last changing for the better.

Robin returned to Tamar House, wondering what lay in store for him. He was deep in thought as he lifted the latch of the strong oak gate and looked up at the lattice windows of his new home. Shoving his hands into the pockets of his new jerkin, he turned towards the door, then stopped dead and swung around. He was sure he had heard a sound.

"Prithee, who is there?" he called.

There was no reply. He stepped forward and stopped once more, as a bird fluttered noisily from under the eaves of the house, startled by something or someone. Then, as the graceful bird soared, so did Robin's spirits, for he had recognized with delight the familiar scent of lavender and rose.

# Glossary

| | |
|---|---|
| annulment | a declaration that a marriage has no legal and/or religious standing (page 53) |
| arthritic | suffering from pain and stiffness of the joints (page 24) |
| bilge water | dirty water that collects in the hull of a boat (page 86) |
| casement | a window, or part of a window, hinged to open like a door (page 79) |
| Christendom | Christians and Christian countries of the world (page 73) |
| cipher | a secret or disguised way of writing; a code (pages 44, 107) |
| comfrey | a healing plant (page 28) |
| damask | a woven fabric with a pattern (page 83) |
| doublet | a short, close-fitting man's jacket, with or without sleeves, worn over a shirt and under an outer jacket or jerkin (page 83) |
| Fool | a jester or clown (pages 38–40, 49, 76–77, 104, 106–107) |
| groat | a silver coin of little value (page 52) |

*Glossary*

| | |
|---|---|
| gunwale | the upper edge of the side of a boat (page 90) |
| hose | breeches or short trousers, worn with stockings (pages 37–39, 83) |
| jerkin | a man's jacket (pages 37, 95, 123) |
| jousting | a sport featuring mounted combat between knights with lances (pages 23, 54) |
| kith and kin | friends and family (page 12) |
| lying-in | a time of waiting and rest before the birth of a child (page 20) |
| monarch | a king or queen (pages 5, 8) |
| night slops | the contents of a chamber pot (page 37) |
| null and void | not binding or valid (page 21) |
| pease pudding | a dish of split peas boiled with onions and carrots and mashed (page 116) |
| Protestant | a follower of the reformed churches (that is, not a Roman Catholic) (pages 8, 106) |
| stern | the back end of a boat (page 51) |
| sweetmeat | a sweet or small cake (pages 43, 122) |
| swooned | fainted (page 55) |
| syllabub | a pudding made with milk or cream, flavoured and sweetened (page 122) |
| wet nurse | a woman employed to suckle a child (page 31) |

# Bibliography

Carlton, Charles. *Royal Childhoods*. London: Routledge and Keegan Paul, 1986.

Fraser, Antonia (editor). *The Lives of the Kings and Queens of England*. London: Weidenfeld and Nicolson, 1993.

Fraser, Antonia. *The Six Wives of Henry VIII*. London: Weidenfeld and Nicolson, 1992.

Williams, Neville. *The Life and Times of Elizabeth I*. London: Weidenfeld and Nicolson, 1992.

For books written for younger readers, try:

Lasky, Kathryn. *Elizabeth I, Red Rose of the House of Tudor*. New York: Scholastic Trade, 1999.

Sauvain, Philip. *The Tudors and Stuarts*. East Sussex: Wayland, 1995.

# From the Author

I was born in England, about 32 kilometres from William Shakespeare's birthplace. My love of all things Elizabethan began with visits to the theatre at Stratford-upon-Avon. That fascination with Tudor history has continued over the years, and teaching the subject has been a pleasure for me.

I trained as a primary school teacher in Wales and have pursued further studies, including a degree in Education. I am currently teaching children with special educational needs.

I hope you like A *Rose on the River* and enjoy this escape with me into the past!

Barbara Fletcher

# Discussion Starters

*1.* Why would a friendship between a rich merchant's daughter and a barge boy have been unusual in Tudor England? Why did Elizabeth Tamar try to keep in contact with Robin?

*2.* During Tudor times, most people could not read or write, so Robin's skill was unusual. Do you think it was difficult for people to improve themselves in those days? Why? Do you think Robin would have remained a boatman all his life?

*3.* Robin and Master Tamar were shocked and hurt when they realized what Elizabeth had done. Should she have thought of them when she made her plans? How might she have justified her attack on Robin?

*4.* Why would the royal household think that silence was better than trying to pursue and punish those responsible for the kidnap plot?